KARL'S PASSAGE

AUTUMNVILLE SERIES BOOK ONE

K WENDT

This book is a work of fiction. Places, events, and situations in this story are purely fictional. Any resemblance to actual persons, living or dead, is purely coincidental.

ISBN   978-1-956581-05-8   HB
ISBN   978-1-956581-04-1   PB
ISBN   978-1-005188-29-0   EB
ASIN   B09RTLXCTS

ERIN GO BRAGH Publishing
Canyon Lake, TX
www.ErinGoBraghPublishing.com

CHAPTER ONE

Karl had just finished checking out a customer when his cell phone dinged. He walked to his office in the back and saw it was a message from his mom, Judy.

The hair on the back of his neck raised slightly as he read the simple two-word text: "Call me." He sat down in the black rolling chair behind his desk and dialed. The phone had barely had time to ring when she answered.

"Hey, Mom," Karl started to say.

"Karl," she spoke with a shaky voice, "your dad had a heart attack."

Karl slumped in his chair. He knew his dad hadn't been feeling well lately. "I'll be there by tonight," he said without hesitation.

Karl was the middle child of his parents' three children. Karl and his older brother, Michael, helped run the family chain of bookstores in Upstate New York. Karl worked at the one in Spires, Michael manned the one in Maple, and their dad, Peter, ran the original in Shale.

"Okay, good," his mom said. "Could you call Michael and tell him? I can't get ahold of him."

Karl sighed, told his mom he would, and hung up. He found Michael's name in his phone and hit the call button, putting it on speaker while he gathered his things. The call went to voicemail.

"Hey, Big Brother," Karl said, "now isn't the time to ignore Mom. Dad's had a heart attack. Call her."

He ended the call and started toward the front of the store. He didn't care about the way he had just told Michael about their dad. Michael had always had some sort of weird grudge against the family and wouldn't speak to any of them, not even to his sister, Stacy, who lived in North Carolina.

Janice, who managed the store for Karl, was at the front counter entering new inventory.

"Janice," Karl went around the counter, "I need to go to Shale for a few days. My dad had a heart attack."

Janice stopped what she was doing. "Oh my gosh! Is Mr. Robertson, okay?"

"I'm not sure what his condition is right now, but I'm heading out so I can get there this evening."

"Okay, I'll let everyone here know," Janice assured.

"I appreciate that," Karl sighed. "I'll call you tomorrow so we can go over a few things for the store."

"Sure, Karl," Janice picked up the inventory sheet. "I'll take care of everything. Keep me posted on your dad."

"Thanks."

Ten minutes later, Karl was packing in his loft, three blocks from the store. Most days, he walked to work since he lived so close, but that day he was thankful he'd taken his motorcycle.

His phone buzzed in his pocket as he went about grabbing things to throw into his bag. He didn't know how long he would be gone but being only a couple of hours away meant he could make quick trips back if necessary.

"Hey," he spoke into the phone.

"Hey," Felicia began "You sound out of breath."

"I'm kind of in a hurry," he told her. "I need to get on the road. Dad had a heart attack."

"Oh, Karl, I'm so sorry. How long will you be gone?"

"I'm not sure yet, but Janice is going to run the store for me."

"Okay, dear," Felicia began, "just don't forget about our lunch plans with Mom and Dad on Sunday."

Karl stopped packing long enough to process what she had said. "Felicia," he tried to say kindly, "I don't know that I will be able to make lunch on Sunday. I don't know how bad Dad is, but he and my mom are a little more important right now."

"Well, of course, Karl." He could hear the pouting in her voice. "I just don't want to stand my parents up."

"I'm sure they'll understand. I have to go."

Karl maneuvered his way out of the city twenty minutes later, after calling his mom to let her know he was on his way.

As he settled into the drive before him, he thought about his conversation with Felicia. That wasn't the first time she had brushed off something important to him. But she hadn't always been like that. The Felicia he had dated was carefree and kind. The Felicia he had been dealing with since the engagement, though, was aggressive and almost mean. All of a sudden, everything had to be her way, and there were constant questions about the business. Karl didn't like that he was going to have to address her behavior the next time they were together.

His thoughts drifted to Michael. He didn't understand his older brother at all. Michael always acted like the world was out to get him, when, in reality, he had always gotten everything he wanted. Michael was always trying to keep up with the Joneses. He didn't seem to understand happiness didn't exist in material things. And relationships eluded him.

Their parents never spoiled them as they grew up. Both boys and their sister had to help with the bookstore. Instead of allowances, they got paychecks. Karl and Stacy learned the value of earning a dollar and being able to support themselves. Michael always squandered his earnings on the next big thing.

Two hours later, Karl parked at the hospital and went to the information counter to find out which room his dad was in. Peter was in the ICU on the third floor.

When Karl stepped out of the elevator, he followed the signs to the ICU and asked a nurse where he could find Peter Robertson's room.

"He's in the second room to your right, but you'll have to wait to go in," the nurse told him. "There is someone with him right now."

Disappointed to have to wait a little bit longer, Karl found a chair near his father's door. He picked up a magazine from the table beside him and flipped through it until he heard the door click open.

"Karl," Judy called as she walked out.

Karl stood up and hugged his mom, "How's he doing?"

"Okay, I guess," Judy answered. "They assure me he's only in here until all the tests come back. They're keeping him sedated until they know exactly what all has happened."

"Mom," Karl began, "what did happen?"

"Why don't you go in and see your father for a minute?" Judy suggested. "Then, when you've finished your visit, we can talk."

Judy sat down. Karl knew his mom wasn't just suggesting what should be done. She was directing what would be done. She had always been a strong woman, and her husband's sudden illness didn't alter that one bit. If anything, it strengthened it.

Karl went into the room his father was sleeping in. Tubes were going into his body and wires were attached to his chest, making the machines beside his bed beep. The Peter he knew was just as strong and able-bodied as Judy. The man before him looked pale and weak, like he barely had any strength left for anything. Karl couldn't stand to see his father that way and left the room.

"You weren't in there very long," his mother noted.

"It's hard to see him like that."

Judy wrapped her arm around her son's. "I know, dear. Trust me, I know. Let's go get a coffee."

It was almost ten o'clock when Michael decided to call his mom. Karl stayed in his parents' living room while his mom walked into the kitchen as she spoke into the phone. The call lasted all of five minutes.

"That was your brother," Judy came back into the living room. "He won't be able to come down for a while. Apparently, the bookstore is too busy for him to leave right now."

Karl rolled his eyes inwardly. Michael's store wasn't any more profitable than his or his dad's. Big Brother just didn't want to be around family, and coming to see his dad would force him to.

CHAPTER TWO

Michael paced the tiny kitchen of his apartment as his dinner burned. "I told you. I don't have the cash right now," he argued into his phone.

"Then I suggest you find a way to get it," the voice on the other end responded.

Click.

Michael let out the breath he had been holding since the first ring of the phone. They had been after him for weeks to pay back his loan. Only, with their particular interest rate, Michael didn't have the cash they were asking for.

How could he? The store was barely above water, thanks to his gambling habits. Michael began moving money around the different accounts a couple of months ago to cover his first debt with the bookie. He had been on a roll with his winnings in the races until he bet on the wrong guy. He was in thousands of dollars over his head.

And his dad was in the hospital, recovering from a heart attack. He knew that as the oldest child he was expected to be there, but with his bookie constantly hassling him for money, he couldn't go just yet. He couldn't let his mom or even Karl know what was going on.

The tone in his mom's voice told him she wasn't happy that he wasn't on his way. What could he do though? He had to get out from under his debt first. Dad is going to be okay, he rationalized. Mom doesn't seem too worried about him. Michael just needed a couple more days and then he would do his duty as the oldest and be there for his parents. He just had to make a call, and then he was sure everything would be taken care of.

Karl kissed his mom goodnight and went upstairs to his old bedroom. He threw his bag on the desk chair he used to spend hours on while studying. Even though he followed his dad's and Michael's footsteps in being a part of the family business, Karl had chosen to go to college and earn a business degree. He had felt he would have a better chance of running a successful store with that knowledge combined with learning under his dad. Karl's store was the top performer of the three, and he took pride in that.

Rummaging through his bag, Karl pulled out his toiletry bag, walked into the bathroom, found a fresh towel, and pulled back the shower curtain. Smiling, he noticed that his mom had made sure, as always, that his favorite shampoo and soap were on the shower shelves. He turned on the water and by the time he was undressed, the small bathroom was starting to fill with steam.

Most of the time, a hot shower would help Karl clear his head, but that night he found it uninviting as he lathered up and rinsed off. He was too emotionally drained to let the water calm him.

Checking his phone before climbing into bed, Karl saw that he had two messages—one Felicia and one from Michael. He opened Felicia's first, hoping it was an apology for the conversation earlier. Instead, it was a reminder about lunch with her parents on Sunday. It was Thursday night; he doubted he would make it. He scrolled down to his brother's message. Again, he was disappointed. Michael wrote that he was glad Karl was there with their mom and that he would try to be there soon. Karl shut his phone off and put it on the charger. He had had enough for one day and he lay down in bed, hoping it wouldn't take long to fall asleep.

Two hours later, Karl lay in the bed, staring up at the ceiling. There was too much on his mind to sleep. While Felicia and Michael were part of the thoughts running through his mind, Karl wondered about all the what-ifs of his dad's situation. What if Dad is paralyzed and can't run the store? What if Dad has to be moved into assisted living? What if Dad doesn't make it?

Karl ran a possible scenario with each thought, feeling that creating a tentative plan would calm him down and help him sleep. Instead, each scenario created more possible problems, forcing him to create plans for those.

It was two in the morning. Karl knew his mother would be up in four hours, getting ready to go back to the hospital. He threw the covers off and found his old radio on the desk. He tuned it to his favorite station and had it play softly as he climbed back into bed. That trick used to work for him all the time when he couldn't sleep. He hoped it still did.

CHAPTER THREE

Judy was trying not to make a lot of noise in the kitchen so Karl could sleep for a while even though she was anxious to get to the hospital. Her two-story home was beautiful, but the sound of clanging pots and pans was as loud upstairs as it was in the kitchen.

Her hands shook as she poured herself a second cup of coffee. She was still in shock from the previous day's events.

Peter had decided to stay home because he didn't feel well. That alone told Judy something wasn't right. Peter never missed work unless he was too ill to get out of bed.

That day was different though. He seemed fine when he first got out of bed, just moved a little slower than normal. When Judy talked to him over breakfast, he had a hard time focusing; that wasn't like him at all. Peter had always had a sharp mind and a quick wit. He claimed he was just a little more tired than normal and went up to take a shower.

Judy was putting the breakfast dishes in the dishwasher when she heard a loud thump above her. She turned off the water in the sink and ran upstairs, not expecting to see her husband passed out on the bathroom floor.

It took the ambulance twenty minutes to get there. In that time, Judy tried desperately to get Peter to talk to her, but he remained unresponsive. Even when she and Karl left the hospital, Peter still had not woken up and spoken to her.

Holding her coffee in one hand, she picked up the morning paper off the counter and walked over to the small round table in the corner. She sat down in her usual chair that looked out through the glass door into their lush backyard.

Judy was trying to attempt some normalcy even though inwardly she was scared to death for her husband and for herself. She wasn't ready to live alone or to be a widow. Judy shook those thoughts out of her head. Peter was a strong and healthy man, always had been. He will be okay, she told herself as she attempted to drink her coffee and read the paper.

Karl came into the kitchen an hour later and found his mom at the table, staring out into the yard.

"Morning, Mom," he walked up to the coffee pot.

Judy took a minute to respond. "You'll have to warm your coffee in the microwave," she told him. "The coffee maker turned itself off thirty minutes ago."

"Okay." Karl took a cup from the cabinet and poured coffee into it. Though it still seemed to be warm, he did as he was told and warmed it up in the microwave.

"What would you like for breakfast?" Judy asked.

"I'm not all that hungry. I can make a bowl of cereal for myself."

11

"Are you sure that will be enough?" Judy asked. "I'm not sure how long we'll be at the hospital today and who knows what the cafeteria food is like there."

He joined her at the table with his coffee. "Yes, Mom, it'll be plenty."

"Okay, then," she got up from the table. "I think I'll go upstairs and get ready."

Karl stood in front of the glass door his mother had been staring through. It was February, and the ground outside seemed to betray what time of year it was. Looking out into the yard both his parents took so much pride in, he wondered if his dad would be able to continue helping his mom with it.

Downing his coffee, Karl decided the what-ifs didn't matter at the moment. What was important was his dad getting well. Karl put his coffee cup in the sink and grabbed a box of bran flakes from the pantry, a bowl and spoon from the cabinet, and the milk from the fridge and went to the table to eat. He knew his mother would fuss if he didn't eat something, and like she said, neither of them knew what the day entailed.

By that evening, Peter had shown no sign of improvement. The doctors didn't seem to be hopeful and had suggested that Judy and Karl start looking at hospice care. Karl stood back while his mom argued with the doctors about keeping Peter in the ICU a few more days.

Karl and Judy picked up chicken in a fast-food drive-through on the way home. Neither of them had the energy to cook supper.

Once in the kitchen, Karl and Judy went through the motions, getting plates, glasses, and utensils out and then sitting down to eat. Karl was taking a bite of his second piece of chicken when his mom finally spoke.

"I'm not ready to give up on your father," she whispered.

Karl froze, holding his chicken in midair. "I didn't ask you to."

Judy pushed her barely touched plate away. "I know, but I feel like the doctors have."

Karl put down his chicken and pushed his own plate away. "Mom, the doctors deal with things like this every day. Wouldn't you rather they be up-front with us about what they believe is best for Dad than lead us on?" he asked.

"I know they mean well, but Peter isn't their husband. They haven't spent the last forty-odd years with him. I can't just let him go."

Karl could see his mother's eyes tearing up. A decision had to be made, and his mom was in no state to make it. "Why don't we finish dinner and then call Michael and Stacy?" he suggested. "Let's discuss this as a family before we make any rash decisions."

Judy seemed to relax a bit at the suggestion and pulled her plate back toward her. "Okay, we'll call right after we eat."

CHAPTER FOUR

Karl awoke early Sunday morning to the sound of his phone ringing. Still trying to wake up, he swatted his hand toward the phone and picked it up.

"Hello," he murmured with his eyes still closed.

"Good morning, sweetie," the voice on the other end chimed. "Are you ready for today?"

Karl's eyes shot open. It was Felicia. He'd forgotten to call her and cancel lunch. "Good morning, Felicia," Karl sat up.

"You didn't answer my question. Are you ready to have lunch with my parents today?"

"Felicia," Karl took a breath as he tried to choose his words carefully, "I'm still at my parents' house. My dad isn't doing well."

"What!" Felicia's voice echoed through the phone. "Karl, you know how important today is to me."

"I understand that, but my mom needs me here right now."

"Karl, it's only seven." He could hear an attempt to change her tone as she spoke. "You could still make it for lunch."

He couldn't believe how Felicia was acting. Can't she see that family is more important than a lunch date?

"Felicia, please apologize to your parents for me, but I'm not going to be able to make it. I need to stay here a few more days."

He waited to see if she would respond. When she didn't, he added, "I love you. Have a good time with your parents."

"Bye, Karl" was all she could reply before she hung up.

By Sunday afternoon, Karl and his mother were waiting for Michael to arrive. Both boys would attend meetings with their mom and then Karl would update Stacy, so everyone would understand what was going on before a decision was made to put Peter in hospice care. Waiting allowed Judy more time to assess the situation and, they hoped, the extra time Peter needed to improve.

As of that morning, Peter's condition remained unchanged. Karl worried for both his dad and his mom. As much as he wanted his dad to get better, Karl didn't want him to keep suffering, and he wasn't sure his mom's strong exterior could handle losing her husband slowly. He felt bad for it, but in some ways, Karl wished Peter would go ahead and pass on. Then no one would have to continue suffering.

Michael pulled into the driveway and sat in his four-door economy car for a minute before shutting the engine off. He didn't want to be there and have to voice his opinion on what should be done, not that he didn't care. He loved his family very much, but he and Karl had been born out of order. Karl had always been better at filling the big brother-oldest child role.

Michael threw his head back and closed his eyes. He wasn't a praying man, but he found himself asking God to please keep his family from finding out anything. Taking a deep breath, Michael got out of his car. He hesitated before grabbing the bag he had packed from the back seat. He was hoping he would be able to head back to Maple today.

As he stepped through the front door, Michael sensed an eerie quiet in the house. "Mom," he called out. "Karl."

"In here," Karl replied from the living room.

Michael walked down the long, narrow hallway to the large opening on the left. He found his mom and brother sitting on the couches in the living room as though they had been waiting for him all day. Judy got up and went over to him.

"Michael," she hugged him, "I'm so glad you're here."

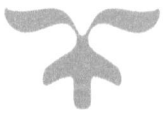

CHAPTER FIVE

Karl got up and gave his brother a light hug. "I'm glad you were able to come."

"How's Dad doing?" Michael asked.

Judy sighed. "Not good."

"We saw him this morning, but we were waiting for you before we went back." Karl watched Michael's shoulders tense as he spoke. *Does Michael really think he can get away without seeing Dad?* He thought. "Mom and I decided to wait for you here so we could all go together."

"Oh," Michael said, "I thought you already did that."

Karl tried to hold his temper. "Mom told you that we would wait until you were here."

Judy put her hands up between her two sons. "Boys, stop fussing," first looking at Karl and then at Michael. "Your father is what is important here. So, please, let's all go and see what the doctors have to say."

The meeting with the doctors was ineffective as far as Karl was concerned. They already had their minds made up that they couldn't do anything else for Peter. Karl watched his mom struggle during the meeting. She wasn't ready to let her husband go.

Karl paced the hall while Michael and his mom visited Peter. He was too agitated about the whole situation to see his dad. Decisions had to be made, and Karl knew Michael wouldn't have any part in it. Even though he was the oldest child, Michael never helped in making family decisions. Karl had been surprised when his mom had asked Michael to come and be a part of the decision. He wasn't sure what prompted her to do that.

The door to his father's room clicked open, and Judy and Michael joined Karl in the hall.

"How about we go somewhere for an early dinner?" Judy stated more than asked.

"I really need to get on the road," Michael spoke.

"I thought you were at least staying the night," Judy scolded.

"Well," Michael shifted uncomfortably from one foot to the other, "I brought an overnight bag just in case, but it would be better if I went back tonight."

"Michael," Judy's cheeks flushed pink, "we need to discuss what we need to do. I would prefer you at least stay overnight. I don't know what could be more important to you right now."

"So, where do you want to go eat, Mom?" Karl asked, attempting to stop an argument from happening in the hospital hallway.

CHAPTER SIX

Later in the evening, Karl walked across the hall to Michael's old room. He knocked lightly on the closed door before turning the knob to go in.

"Look," Michael was saying into his phone as he turned to see Karl, "can we talk about this later? My family is in a bit of a crisis right now."

Karl skimmed his brother's room while he waited for the call to end. Like his room, Michael's hadn't changed since he had moved out years ago.

Michael put his phone on the nightstand beside his bed. "What's up?" he asked.

"We need to make a decision about Dad," Karl declared.

"I don't think Mom wants to," Michael answered.

"She doesn't," Karl tried to keep his breath even. "That's why we have to."

"Oh, no, Little Brother. I'm not signing off on Dad's death unless Mom says to."

"Mom isn't going to be ready for a long time, if she ever is," Karl said, "and Dad is suffering. It's not fair to ask him to keep suffering."

19

Karl got up early the next morning and waited for his mom and brother to come down for coffee. He had made a decision during the night, when he couldn't sleep again, to take charge of the situation. He knew he would have to corner Michael first thing.

Karl was looking out into the yard from the glass door. He turned to the entranceway when he heard footfalls on the stairs.

"Well, good morning, Karl," Judy acknowledged. "Didn't expect to see you up yet."

"I had trouble sleeping and gave up a couple of hours ago, so I worked out in the basement, took a shower, and made some coffee," he answered as he walked toward the coffee pot. "Want some?"

"Yes, please," Judy took her place at the breakfast table and began to fumble with the morning paper, already opened and laid out. "I haven't been sleeping all that well either."

A few minutes later, they were joined by Michael, who didn't appear to be fully awake yet. He was like a bull in a china shop as he fumbled through the cabinets looking for a coffee cup. Karl got up to help Michael so the clanging would stop. Without saying a word, Karl grabbed a cup, poured coffee in it, handed it to his brother, and went back to the table. Michael joined Karl and Judy at the table after downing his cup and refilling it.

"Looks like none of us slept very well last night," Judy noted.

Michael grunted an inaudible response.

Karl took a deep breath. "We need to decide what to do."

"Could you wait until I'm fully awake before we talk about it, Little Brother?" Michael asked.

Karl looked at Michael, who only called him Little Brother when he was annoyed or angry.

"No," Karl said, "we can't keep putting it off."

"Let's make breakfast," Judy suggested. "Once we've eaten, we'll discuss what we think is best to do for your father."

Karl slumped in his chair in defeat. Michael continued sipping his coffee and looking at the newspaper. Judy got up and started pulling out the ingredients to make pancakes. Karl gathered plates, forks, napkins, butter, and syrup to put on the table.

Breakfast was eaten in silence except for the occasional clanking of forks on plates. Once everyone was finished and the dishes were in the sink, Karl ushered his mom and Michael into the living room. He stood in the doorway so neither of them could leave the room. Michael and Judy sat on the sage-colored couch facing Karl.

"I know we don't want to talk about this," Karl began, "but we have to. The doctors haven't given us a choice."

"Karl," Judy said softly, "I just don't know that I can make that decision. In a way, it makes me feel like I'm killing your father by putting him in hospice and not letting him continue to fight for himself." She looked at both of her sons. "You know your father has always been a proud and stubborn man. I don't feel right waving the white flag of surrender for him."

"Mom," Karl started, "the doctors claim dad doesn't have the strength to fight anymore."

The phone rang on the table next to Michael. "Hello, this is Michael Robertson." Michael waited for the person on the other end to finish talking. "Thank you. We'll be there as soon as we can."

"Who was that?" Karl asked.

"The hospital. Dad made the decision for us. He passed away a few minutes ago."

CHAPTER SEVEN

"Thanks for coming to the funeral, Felicia," Karl started once they were back at his parents' house.

"Well, of course, Karl," Felicia huffed. "Why wouldn't I be here?"

"I just thought you were tied up getting ready for the spring arrivals," he told her.

"Clothes can always wait, Karl," Felicia answered. "Besides, I know how much your parents mean to you."

Karl felt the direct hit of her words. Felicia was still angry with him for cancelling lunch with her and her parents.

"How many times do I have to tell you I'm sorry for cancelling on you and your parents?" he asked, trying to keep his anger at bay. "My father was dying. I've never known you to be so coldhearted."

He walked away before Felicia had a chance to respond. He was starting to have doubts about marrying her, especially after how she'd behaved since his dad's heart attack. Forty-eight hours hadn't even passed since his father's death, and Felicia was already asking who would take primary ownership of the chain of stores. Karl wondered if Felicia had always been all about the money and he just had been too blind to see it before.

"Hello, Michael," Felicia walked up and hugged him. "I'm sorry for your loss. Maybe betting on the races isn't a good idea for you right now." Felicia flashed Michael a wicked smile.

"Really, Felicia," Michael finally said. "Not here. Not now. Don't you have any respect for your fiancé and our family in our time of mourning?"

"Oh, come on, Michael. We both know you're more interested in getting whatever money you can from Peter's death so you can pay your debts and keep gambling."

Michael grabbed her arm and pulled her closer to him. "That's enough Felicia. Today isn't the day to remind me of how shallow I am. Now, if you'll excuse me, I'm going to get something to drink. Why don't you straighten up and go be a good little fiancée to my brother?"

Felicia jerked her arm away. "Fine, but you better remember our deal."

"I'm sure you won't let me forget," he told her. "What Karl sees in you, I'll never know."

Stacy had witnessed the entire encounter between Michael and Felicia from across the living room. Something was going on between them, and from what Stacy could tell, it wasn't anything good.

Karl was in the kitchen talking to some of his parents' friends when Stacy found him. She stood beside him quietly, waiting for the conversation to end. When the friends moved on, Karl draped an arm around Stacy's shoulders.

"How are you doing, Sis?" he asked.

"I'm okay," she answered. "How are you?"

"Hanging in there," he admitted. "There's still a lot to do."

"It doesn't all have to be done today," Stacy added. "Remember that."

Karl smiled at his little sister. They had always been close. "I know, but someone has to help Mom," he told her.

"Make Michael do it," she snapped and then quickly regretted it. "I'm sorry, Karl. It would just be nice if he did his brotherly duties for once."

"I know, but that's just not who he is."

"You're too kind, Karl."

"Maybe so, Sis, but all I know is that Mom needs help and at least one of us should help her. Who helps her doesn't really matter."

Michael came into the kitchen.

"What are you looking for?" Karl asked him.

"A beer," Michael answered as he looked into the fridge.

"You know there isn't any beer here, Michael," Stacy told him. "Mom and Dad don't drink that stuff."

"Dad had one every now and then," Michael closed the fridge door. "I thought maybe there would be one in here still."

"Michael, it's barely lunchtime. Why do you need a beer now?" Karl asked.

"It's my way of coping, Little Brother. We can't all be perfect like you."

"What's that supposed to mean?" Karl asked a little too loud. Lowering his voice, he growled, "Don't make a scene here, Michael. Don't embarrass mom like that."

Michael rolled his eyes. "Yeah, yeah, whatever, Little Brother," he muttered and walked out of the kitchen.

"Sometimes I'm amazed we're related to him," Karl sighed.

Stacy stayed quiet. She didn't much care for Michael's behavior either, and she was curious about what was going on between Michael and Felicia, but it wasn't the time to worry about it.

CHAPTER EIGHT

The family had arranged to meet with their lawyer the day after Peter's funeral.

Stacy had to be home by Sunday because her husband, John, had to leave for a business trip Monday morning and someone had to be home for their kids, and Michael was chomping at the bit to get back to Maple. Karl seemed to be the only one willing and able to stay with Judy.

Judy sat down at her vanity and thought about her kids as she took her time dressing for the meeting. They were all good in their own ways, even Michael with all his struggles had some good in him. She wasn't upset that Stacy couldn't stay longer. She understood Stacy needed to be home to tend to her own family.

Judy pulled a tissue from the box sitting on the corner and dabbed her eyes. She did wish Stacy lived closer though. I could sure use some time with my grandchildren right now, she thought. Maybe in a few days I'll take a trip down to Autumnville to see them.

Taking a deep breath, Judy looked at herself in the vanity mirror. How am I going to continue life without Peter? she thought. He was my rock. He was the family's rock.

Karl was a lot like Peter in that respect. Judy was very thankful her middle son was able to be with her these last few weeks. Becoming the voice of reason was be a hard thing for anyone in that situation, but Karl seemed to know what had to be done.

He was the more level-headed and business-minded of her two boys. Peter had been so proud when Karl's store outsold his. Karl had always been the logical choice in her eyes to take over the family business. She believed Karl wanted that as well. Hopefully, feelings wouldn't be hurt today with the reading of Peter's will.

The four of them took their seats nervously as Kyle Boyd, the family's lawyer, made his way around his desk to begin the grueling task of reading Peter's will.

"Good morning, everyone," he began. "I wish we were meeting under different circumstances."

As the Robertson family mumbled their good mornings, Kyle eyed each of them briefly. Judy was sitting up straight in her chair, wringing a tissue in her hands. Karl and Stacy were on either side of her. Stacy's hand rested on Judy's forearm while Karl sat back in his chair and turned his attention to the floor. Michael was the only one that appeared laid-back as though this were just another business meeting.

"Kyle," Judy said softly, "if you don't mind, could we forego the formalities and get right into things? I think we would all rather have some time alone at the house."

Kyle gave Judy a sympathetic smile. "Sure, Judy."

He opened the file before him and began reading Peter's last will and testament. He quickly went over the little items, like certain pieces of jewelry and Peter's tools in the shed behind their house before getting to the chain of bookstores.

"As to the chain of bookstores," Kyle began slowly, "Peter stated that he was very pleased with how both Michael and Karl were able to run the stores they were in charge of, especially when Karl's outsold the one here. Peter also stated that he knew Judy didn't want to be in charge of the bookstores but would like to still earn what residual income she could from them. While both of you boys have strong yet different attributes that have helped you in succeeding with your stores, Peter's wish was to follow the traditional standard and have Michael take over the role of overseeing all three stores, as he is the oldest child."

Kyle caught a quick smile from Michael before he managed to hide it. Karl then sat up in his seat, shocked by the decision his dad had made.

"Was that really what Dad wanted to do?" Karl asked his mom.

"Yes, Karl," she said. "Your father was very adamant that Michael be the one to take over if something happened to him."

"Why?" was all that Karl could manage to say.

Judy patted Karl's hand. "It wasn't anything against you, Karl. Your father was very proud of everything you had accomplished with your store, but he was also very old-school when it came to family tradition, and he believed in passing it on to the oldest child first."

Kyle cleared his throat. "In the event Michael is unable to perform his duties as overseer of the chain of bookstores, Karl is to step into the role."

"What?" Michael was shocked. "Who determines that?" he demanded.

"I'm to monitor the books for the first three months," Kyle answered. "If you show you're able to handle this position, it's yours to keep."

Michael adjusted himself in his seat. He was stiff, worried about his chances to keep the position his father had promoted him to.

Kyle stood up. "That's all there is in the will," he said.

"Thank you, Kyle," Judy said. "I'm sure we'll be in touch."

Kyle came around the desk and shook everyone's hands as they headed out the door, not letting on that he didn't agree with Peter's decision about the family business. Kyle didn't know Michael very well, but there was something about him that gave Kyle a bad vibe. That's why he had pushed Peter so hard for that three-month trial clause. Even Peter had to know that putting the business in Michael's hands was a risky venture.

CHAPTER NINE

Karl stewed in the driver's seat of his mom's SUV as he drove everyone back to the house. He didn't understand why his dad would have Michael take over the business. Karl didn't know how well Michael's bookstore was doing, but he had assumed through conversations with his dad, that the store in Spires was more profitable.

Karl didn't want Michael's store to fail, but when his big brother was put in charge of something, it usually crumbled. Maybe Karl was underestimating Michael. Maybe Michael was actually doing a good job running his store. No matter how much he didn't like it, Karl had to accept that it was his dad's wish for Michael to take over.

In the back seat, Michael was beginning to feel sick. The news from this morning's meeting was tearing up his stomach. When Kyle first announced that Michael was to take over Peter's position, Michael had been happy. All his worries about his debt would go away. But with Kyle monitoring the books, Michael didn't know if he would be able to hide his addiction like he had been. He wrapped his arms tight around his waist as he thought about what it would mean for him if his family found out he'd been cheating the books for years.

Stacy was livid, and knowing she couldn't do anything about it made her angrier. How could Dad do that to Karl? she wondered. He was the obvious choice between her two brothers. Screw tradition! Stacy kept her gaze out the window as they headed to their parents' house. She couldn't stand to look at Michael sitting beside her, and if she looked at Karl, she was going to cry. She was thankful to be sitting behind her mom, though she had no idea how she felt about all of this.

Judy sat in the passenger seat and focused on the scenery. She wondered what her kids were all thinking. Karl was agitated. He had been running his hand through his hair since they left the lawyer's office. Judy knew that was his tell when he was upset. Michael didn't look so well, either, she noticed when she turned her gaze toward him. He looked frightened. Good, she thought. He had never had such an important role before. Maybe it would help him finally straighten up.

Judy was no dummy. She knew Peter had bailed Michael out of a couple of small gambling debts in the past. Judy was thankful Kyle had insisted on the three-month trial clause. She had always believed that position should go to Karl if something happened to Peter, but Peter had insisted it go to Michael. He said it would crush Michael's ego to be passed over, and Peter had always had a soft spot for Michael.

Judy would stand by Peter's wishes, even if she disagreed with them. Judy had supported her husband in life and she would continue to support him in death. Peter had never given her any reason to doubt his decisions. Hopefully, that wouldn't change with Michael in charge.

CHAPTER TEN

Karl was doing his best to get his life back to normal in Spires. Janice had done a good job running the bookstore for him while he had been gone. He knew she would. She had been his manager for five years and was always willing to help where needed.

Things appeared to be getting back to normal with Felicia, but Karl still had an underlying feeling that things had changed between them. Felicia had been disappointed by the news that Michael was taking over Peter's position instead of Karl. At first, Karl thought she was disappointed for him, but something had changed in her demeanor and she told him that maybe Michael was the best choice after all.

Something about that conversation didn't sit well with Karl. As he headed out to finally have lunch with Felicia and her parents, he wondered if they should stay engaged.

Felicia drummed her fingers lightly on the table as she sat with her parents waiting for Karl to arrive. He was five minutes late. That wasn't like him, but then, he hadn't been the same since his father's heart attack.

Peter not putting Karl in charge of overseeing the three stores had been a bit of a shock, but Felicia decided she could probably handle having Michael in that position due to the current arrangement she had with him.

"Well, look who made it," Felicia's dad, Paul stood up to greet Karl.

"Sorry I'm late," Karl shook Paul's hand. "Apparently, everybody decided to go out to eat at the same time today," he hugged Barbara, Felicia's mom, and then Felicia. "I've never seen traffic so bad here."

He tried to kiss Felicia before sitting down, but she turned away and sat back down. Karl knew that meant she was upset with him again. Ugh! I just can't win with her lately! he thought.

Their May wedding was just a little over a month away. Karl wondered if they would make it that far.

CHAPTER ELEVEN

Michael's palms were sweating. Kyle was expected to come to the store here in Maple to see how Michael was doing in his new role.

Michael had spent the first couple of weeks after his dad's death at the store in Shale, learning about the different things Peter did to keep track of all three stores. He had found some documents that had notes with big question marks on them and had taken those papers home to take a closer look at them. What he discovered shocked him. He was hoping no one else knew about those documents.

This was Kyle's first time to come check on Michael's progress, and Michael was nervous about the possibility of Kyle asking to see those documents. They were locked away in Michael's safe in his apartment.

Hearing the store's door chime, Michael wiped his palms on his pants for the tenth time. Taking a breath, he stood up from his office chair to see if it was Kyle who had come in. He couldn't wait to get that meeting over with.

Judy paced her kitchen holding her third cup of coffee for the day. It was cold in the mug between her hands. She was anxious as she waited for the call.

Once all three of her children had left, Judy had called Kyle and told him to keep her in the loop about everything concerning the bookstores. Judy didn't trust Michael's ability to take over Peter's role.

She was ashamed of herself for feeling that way about her own son, but even with the time he took to stay and learn while he was there, she didn't think he could handle the pressure.

Judy knew her son had a weakness for money. He could never seem to have enough even though he was paid plenty. For some reason, Michael never seemed to grasp the importance of success and financial stability for the future. He always had to take care of the minute he was standing in, not thinking about how it could affect the minute that followed. How could someone with a trait like that be effective as an overseer for three bookstores? Judy just didn't think it was possible.

The phone finally rang a few minutes later. Judy placed her cup in the sink, answered, and listened to what Kyle had to say. Michael was doing okay in his new role, according to Kyle. She said goodbye and went about washing the cup in the sink.

Something nagged at Judy. Kyle's tone didn't match his words. What did he find? she wondered. What is he not telling me? Judy didn't used to meddle in the business affairs between her husband and sons, but she wished she had. She had a strong sensation she wasn't being told the whole truth.

After rinsing the cup for the fifth time, Judy placed it in the drainer beside the sink. She wished the days were warm enough to work in her garden. That always helped her think. Mid-April in New York was still a bit too chilly to enjoy the outdoors for a long period of time. Instead, she went in search of a crochet project she had started for Stacy's daughter, Nicole. That would help her think things out. Keeping her hands busy always helped her mind settle down.

As Kyle drove back to Shale later that day, he thought about the conversations he had had with Peter before his death. Peter had left specific instructions to Kyle pertaining to Michael. Peter knew Michael wasn't the wisest choice to take over his role. He couldn't ignore what he had found. Peter had told Kyle his hope was that by putting Michael in that position that Michael would have to face the truth of what he had done.

Kyle had expected something of that nature to happen when he met with Michael that day. Instead, there was no sign of the documents Peter had discovered just two months prior to his death. Either Michael hadn't found them yet or he was much shrewder than anyone gave him credit for.

Kyle hated that he had to report to Judy. He felt like he was lying to her since Peter had made it clear to Kyle that he didn't want Judy to know anything about what had been going on. Peter had hoped that the issue would be settled by Michael himself.

Kyle didn't see Michael owning up to anything he might have done wrong though. Kyle felt Michael was the typical rich kid who got everything he wanted and was never happy with it.

His next appointment with Michael was in two weeks, right before Karl's wedding. Maybe by then those documents would show up.

CHAPTER TWELVE

Karl's phone rang, causing him to jump from the paperwork he was working on in his office. It was his mom. Karl wasn't sure why, but he was holding his breath as he answered the phone.

"Hello," he said timidly.

"Hello, Karl."

He thought he heard the same timid tone in his mom's voice. Karl let out his breath and asked, "What's going on, Mom?"

"Karl, do you have some time to talk?" Judy asked.

"Yes."

"Better yet," Judy suggested, "can you just come here for a day or two?"

Karl sat up straight in his chair. "What's going on, Mom?" Karl asked firmly.

"It's about the bookstores, Karl," Judy finally said. "I think it would be better for you to come here and hear in person from Kyle and Michael."

"Mom—" Karl began to say, but Judy cut him off.

"Karl, just come here," she said sternly, "now."

"Seriously, Karl," Felicia said over the phone as Karl put a bag together, "is this how it's going to be when we get married? You drop everything and run to your family. We have appointments to get to for our wedding. You have to go to the final fitting for your tux."

Karl took a breath before answering. He couldn't understand why she was reacting that way. "Felicia," he began slowly, "I'm sorry. I have to reschedule the appointments. Surely waiting a couple of days more won't hurt. We still have two weeks until the wedding. I don't know what is going on, but my mother sounded very upset and refused to tell me anything over the phone. The bookstore is my future…and your future. Don't you think I should go find out what is going on?"

Karl heard nothing but silence for a good solid minute. He was starting to think she had hung up on him when she finally spoke.

"You're right. Go. See what is going on and call me as soon as you can."

Karl felt those words were being forced out of her. "Thank you. I love you and I will call you soon," he hung up.

There was no response from Felicia. She just hung up.

Karl thought about Felicia and his relationship with her, as he made the two-hour drive to his mom's house. Something in

Felicia had definitely changed. Or had it? As Karl thought about all the time they had spent together, he realized that there had been hints of this behavior there all along. Felicia had always been selfish. It just took Peter's heart attack for Karl to finally see it. He had always done as Felicia wanted in the relationship, but when it came to what he wanted or needed to do, she had an uncanny way of talking him out of it.

His father's health wasn't an excuse to get away from her. He had needed to be there with his mom. That was his family! He couldn't believe Felicia's coldhearted treatment toward him and his family during that time. She could hold a grudge. He had always known that about her, but to be resentful for not making lunches and appointments when his family was in crisis seemed unreasonable.

By the time Karl arrived at his mom's home, he wasn't so sure he wanted to marry Felicia anymore. He hated himself for feeling that way. Maybe it was just the stress of everything that had happened since February and everything would be better after the wedding. Karl didn't want to walk away from Felicia just yet. Surely, they could work through all this.

He turned off the engine in his truck, grabbed his overnight bag, and took a deep breath before walking inside.

CHAPTER THIRTEEN

The scene before Karl in the living room did not look good. Judy was sitting on the couch, wringing a tissue so tight her hands were splotched red and white. Kyle sat on the edge of one of the recliners with his hands clasped in front of him, his elbows resting on his knees. Michael was in the recliner opposite Kyle. Karl found his body language hard to read. He was sitting back, almost comfortably in the recliner, his arms on the arm rests as he stared at Judy as if waiting for a response.

No one had noticed Karl standing there. He cleared his throat. Judy looked up and almost ran over to him. She hugged him tightly.

"I'm so glad you were able to come on short notice, Karl," she said.

"It's almost becoming a bad habit," he tried to joke. He took another scan of the other two people in the room. "What's going on?" he asked.

"Why don't you come sit down?" Judy suggested as she led him to the couch.

The air was tense. Karl felt like he could no longer breathe as he took a seat next to his mom. "What's this about, guys?" Karl asked. "Would someone please tell me what is going on already?"

There was no use putting it off any longer. Karl needed to be told what had happened.

"Karl," she began but seemed unable to find the words.

"We're bankrupt," Michael blurted out.

Karl's face went white. He wasn't sure he had heard Michael correctly. "Bankrupt?" he asked. "Who's bankrupt?"

"We are," Michael said. "I made some bad business decisions and lost the business."

Karl was on his feet. He wanted to lunge at his brother. Instead, he moved behind the couch and started pacing, running his hand through his hair.

"You mean you gambled it away," Karl finally blurted out.

"Karl!" Judy scolded.

"Don't Karl me, Mom! We all know good and well that Michael has a gambling problem."

Karl kept pacing. He wanted to beat his brother into admitting that was what had happened. He knew he couldn't do that, though, and just kept pacing.

Everyone was silent as the news fell to the floor with a thud. The only sound was Karl's feet pacing the floor.

"Karl, please stop," Judy finally said. She twisted around to look at him. "We need to discuss what to do from here. It's happened. It can't be undone. We have to figure out how we move forward now."

Karl stopped and looked at his mom. It wasn't her fault they were in this mess. It was Michael's. Karl went back around the couch, sat down, and looked at his big brother with disdain. How could Michael be so careless to let this happen?

"Okay," Karl said. "Why don't we start at the beginning? Someone please explain to me what has happened. How is my store affected by this?"

Again, there was silence.

Finally, Kyle shifted in the recliner and cleared his throat. "I'll try to explain it to you, Karl," he said. "Your dad discovered some things in the books toward the end of last year that didn't quite make sense to him. All the documents in question came from Michael's store. The numbers on Peter's books didn't add up with the numbers on the reports Michael turned in each month. Peter had a feeling Michael was taking store money to cover debts he owed to bookies."

Karl glared at Michael as he listened to Kyle.

"Instead of going to the accountant, your dad came to me to see what could be done," Kyle said.

"Why didn't he go to the accountant?" Karl asked.

"Peter thought there was a possibility that Michael had somehow managed to get the accountant to fudge the books so your father wouldn't see what was going on." Kyle looked at Michael. "I checked into the accountant. She didn't have any idea until about a month ago that there was something funny with the numbers. How Michael managed to manipulate the books so well, I'll never know. Anyway, your father and I were working on those documents, what their origins were, what the true money value involved was, and those types of things when he had his heart attack."

Karl was fuming and finding it hard to stay in his seat. He really wanted to light into Michael. Trying to control himself, he knotted his hands together and asked the two big questions he had been holding onto. "If my father knew this was happening, why didn't he change his will? Why did he leave Michael in charge?"

Kyle's gaze dropped to the floor. "He was supposed to come in and change it the day he had his heart attack."

Karl took a minute and let that sink in, not just for his benefit, but Michael's as well. He hoped his big brother heard what Kyle had just admitted. Their dad had intended to change the will. It should have been Karl taking over Peter's position.

"How is my store affected by this?" Karl finally asked.

Judy took Karl's hands. "Sweetie," she said softly, "it's all lost. The business as a whole is so far in the red now, we have to file bankruptcy and close all three locations just to get back into the black."

Karl couldn't take it anymore. He lunged at Michael, knocking over the chair Michael had been sitting in as Michael fell to the floor with Karl.

"You're a sorry excuse of a person," Karl growled through clenched teeth as he took his anger out on Michael. "You have never cared for anyone except yourself. Now we all have to suffer for your selfishness, and I doubt you even care."

"Karl!" Judy yelled from behind him. "Get off your brother!"

Karl felt himself being pulled off of Michael. Kyle had grabbed his left arm when Karl pulled it back to swing at Michael. Kyle pulled Karl over to the other side of the couch, where he had been sitting.

"Are your debts paid now, Big Brother?" Karl asked as he tried to regain control of himself. "Are *you* still in the red with your bookies?"

"Enough!" Judy shouted as she stood between her sons. She pointed at Karl. "I don't like what has happened any more than you do, but I refuse to watch you behave this way. And you," Judy continued as she turned to face Michael, "I suggest you get all your ducks in a row because the second your brother's wedding is over, you're going to rehab."

"Mo—" Michael started to say.

"No! There will be no excuses. You will either go or you will no longer be welcome in my home, and I have a feeling you're about to lose quite a bit more than money. So if I were you, I wouldn't be so eager to lose my family as well."

Judy left the room then, leaving her two sons both shocked and amazed at the boldness neither of them ever knew their mother had in her.

CHAPTER FOURTEEN

Karl had gone out to the backyard. He needed some time to himself to process what was going on. His business. His livelihood. Gone. Just like that. Instead of getting up and going to a job he loved the next day, he'd be putting a closed sign on the door and packing up inventory. According to Kyle, it would be easiest if all inventory was in one store to sell. Then, the sale of the buildings would go more quickly. Everything was going to the bookstore in Shale so Kyle and Judy could oversee it.

Karl didn't blame them for making that decision. It would be easier, and Michael had proven that he couldn't be trusted. Karl kicked at the ground. How could Michael gamble away our livelihood? How could he be so careless?

Karl knew these questions were pointless. It shouldn't have surprised anyone that it happened. So why did their dad ever think it was okay to put Michael in charge? And when Peter had realized what a mistake that was, why did God stop him from changing the will?

That was what Karl was most angry about. He didn't understand why God was allowing all this to happen. They were a good churchgoing family. They all believed in God, even Michael. So why was God destroying their lives? It just didn't seem right.

Karl's phone began to ring. He pulled it out of his pocket and saw Felicia's name on the screen.

Crap, he thought. "Hey," he said.

"Hey," Felicia replied. "Doesn't sound like it was good news."

"It's not," Karl admitted. He held his breath, waiting for her response.

"What's going on now, Karl?" Felicia groaned.

Karl knew from her tone that this wasn't going to go well. She was furious.

"What do you mean you have to sell the store?" she asked. "And why now? Why right before the wedding?"

"I don't have a choice in the matter," Karl tried to tell her, but she cut him off.

"Don't have a choice in the matter!" Felicia's voice bellowed through the phone. "It's your store, Karl. You'd better have a choice in the matter. I'm not marrying you unemployed!"

Click.

It took Karl a bit to realize Felicia had hung up on him. He ran his fingers through his hair. His whole world was crashing down around him, and he felt like he couldn't do anything about it. On top of everything, his fiancée basically just threatened to cancel the wedding.

Maybe he should let her do that. Maybe they shouldn't get married. Felicia apparently only cared about herself. Not once since February had she asked Karl how he was truly doing with everything. Maybe he would surprise her and cancel the wedding himself. He *could* control that.

"Karl," Judy called from the backdoor, "why don't you come in and have something to eat?"

Karl wasn't sure he wanted to face anyone in his mother's house, but he did find himself suddenly hungry.

"All right," he answered as he headed to the door.

Felicia grabbed the couch pillow next to her and screamed into it. She didn't want her next-door neighbors to hear her, but she had to let her anger out somehow. She couldn't believe what was happening. Her whole comfortable future had been taken away by an idiot in charge. Why did Peter ever leave Michael in charge?

Between Karl owning the bookstore and her job as a designer, they were supposed to live comfortably. No worries. No troubles. She could buy whatever she wanted whenever she wanted because they would have money.

Now, she had no idea what Karl's future looked like, and that worried her. She didn't want to have to struggle to make ends meet. God knows, with taste, she wasn't about to do anything in her life second-class. No, she either needed to find a new job for Karl or leave him before it was too late. Or better yet, maybe she could be both boys' saving grace. Michael did owe her after all.

Michael ignored his phone as it vibrated in his pocket. He had peeked at it when it first went off, just before he sat down to eat with his mom and Karl. He knew the person texting him was impatient, but he needed to focus on his mom and brother.

He didn't blame Karl for being angry with him. If he was honest, he would be angry if Karl had done what he did. His addiction cost them a dream their father had built with his bare hands. For the first time in his life, Michael found gambling disgusting. He had never once thought about how his addiction would affect his family.

Lunch was eaten in silence. Michael barely touched the food on his plate while he watched his mom and Karl. He had hoped maybe they could discuss things better since Kyle wasn't there, but neither Karl nor Judy had anything to say.

"Mom," Michael said finally.

Judy looked up from the sandwich she was eating. "Yes, Michael," she acknowledged.

"I'm sorry, Mom," he spoke carefully. "I never thought there was a chance we would lose the stores."

"I don't understand exactly what all has happened," she said. "I know you're sorry, but that doesn't fix this. You've pulled us into your addiction and now we're suffering for something we didn't do. Once we're done eating, you and I are going to find a rehab for you."

Michael knew better than to argue with his mom. In a way, he was relieved he would be going to rehab. He knew he needed help. Maybe rehab was the answer. Once he was done eating, he rinsed his dishes and set them in the sink. He excused himself and went to his room to read all the text messages that had come in.

He sat on his bed in disbelief. What was she thinking? There was no way that what she suggested would work. Karl would never be okay with Felicia's family owning the stores, and he definitely would not be okay with working as her manager.

CHAPTER FIFTEEN

Karl couldn't believe the day had finally come. Several times during the last few weeks he had thought for sure the wedding would be cancelled. But he was standing in a small room behind the pulpit, waiting for it to be time to take his place at the altar.

The wedding was already running fifteen minutes behind because Felicia had not arrived at the church yet, and while this concerned Karl, he told himself everything was okay. She would be there with her parents any minute.

Michael was pacing nervously beside Karl. Even though they had their differences, there was no one else Karl would have wanted as his best man. A few more minutes passed before there was a knock on the door.

"Finally," Karl went to open the door.

He was surprised to find his mom and sister standing there. Karl glanced down at an envelope in Stacy's hands.

"It's for you," she handed it to him, walking into the room with their mom.

Judy, Michael, and Stacy all found chairs while they waited for Karl to read the note.

"I don't believe it," Karl mulled.

Judy stood up and went over to him, placing a hand on his arm. "What is it, Karl?"

"I've been stood up," he declared simply.

"What!" Michael and Stacy said in unison as they went over to Karl and their mom.

"Felicia isn't coming," Karl said slowly. "She's decided she can't marry a man down on his luck."

"Oh, Karl," Stacy went over to hug him. "I'm so sorry."

Karl hugged her back and pulled away. "It's okay," he tried to keep his emotions in check. "It's for the best, really, especially with everything that has gone on this year."

"I'm so glad we were able to block her from buying the business," Judy said.

"Mom!" Karl was surprised by her words.

"Well, it's true," Judy shrugged. "She's greedy, Karl. She always has been. I tried to love and accept her as a soon-to-be member of the family, but she showed her true colors a little too much. I'm glad you're not marrying her now. That was the best thing she could have ever done for you."

CHAPTER SIXTEEN

Karl settled in for the long drive to Autumnville, North Carolina. He wasn't sure why he was going to his sister's house. He wasn't in the mood to visit anyone. It had been a month since Felicia had left him at the altar and he still didn't feel like seeing anyone.

He had managed somehow to help Janice close down the store in June. Outside of that, he stayed in his apartment. He wanted nothing to do with the outside world or anyone in it, not even family.

His mom and Stacy both tried in the beginning to check on him, but after a while, he stopped answering their calls, only responding here and there through texts until a few days ago, when Stacy basically yelled at him through a voicemail to actually call her. By the end of the conversation, he had reluctantly agreed to visit for a few days.

He was on his way to see Stacy and her family, wishing he had stayed home. In the past, he had loved visiting them. He had always thought Autumnville was a beautiful place, and he enjoyed doing things with his niece and nephew. But he feared any more drama and bad things happening. He couldn't take even one more thing. There's some saying that everything comes in threes. I hope to God that's right, he thought.

Karl laughed at the thought. He'd stopped talking to God the day he was supposed to get married. God had left him, or at least that's how he felt. Why else did all this happen? God had taken away the three most important things to him. As far as Karl was concerned, God could stay gone. He had no use for someone that took your life away from you.

After they had gone through everything with Kyle, it had been clear Michael was too far in the red to keep his place in Maple. He had moved in with his mom two weeks after completing rehab.

Michael would work as a salesperson in the bookstore in Shale until it closed. He would no longer have anything to do with the books, and his paychecks would be deposited into an account that only Kyle had control of to make payments on the debts Michael had accumulated.

Michael sat with Judy, eating breakfast at her kitchen table. "When was Karl going to Stacy's?" Michael asked.

"I think Stacy said today," Judy answered.

"I think it'll be good for him," Michael said. "He can't keep blocking us out."

Judy looked over her cup at Michael. "To be fair, none of what happened was his fault."

Michael winced at his mom's comment. "I know that, Mom, but he can't sulk about it the rest of his life," he said. "I'm very sorry for everything that happened. I know I'm responsible for part of what happened. I can't take it back."

Judy put her cup down and softened her tone. She had forgiven Michael weeks ago. "I know that, Michael. Your brother will come around. He just needs some time,"

CHAPTER SEVENTEEN

Anxiety rose up in Karl's chest as he got closer to Autumnville. He'd basically taken a vacation from people for a month and wasn't sure he had it in him to face anyone yet. He didn't want to be pitied. Truth be told, that was one of the reasons he had been keeping to himself.

At some point, he knew he would forgive his brother for losing the family business. But Felicia had shattered his heart. Even with all the questions he had about whether or not they should get married, he still wanted to marry her.

The note she had so graciously delivered to him on what was supposed to be their wedding day had shocked him. Sure, they had fought more when she had brought up the crazy idea of buying the bookstores and *letting* his family continue to run them as they were. She had claimed it was her way of forgiving Karl for putting off lunch with her parents.

"We're about to be family," she declared. "Best to move on."

It wasn't until later that Karl found out about the loan Felicia had given Michael when their dad was in the hospital. Apparently, in his desperation to pay off his bookie for his bad gamble, Michael had called Felicia and begged her to help him.

If Karl had known Michael needed money that bad, he would have helped him. Who knew Felicia would hold the loan over his head and try to con her way into owning the business? She had tried to give Michael an ultimatum—pay back her loan or sell his share to her for less than it was worth to cover his debts.

Luckily, Michael had been with Karl and his mom and had confessed what was going on to them. Karl had called Felicia on the spot and told her not to interfere and that he was disappointed in her. It had really upset Karl that she had stooped so low.

He thought they had gotten past all that, though, when he went back to Spires to start packing up the store and getting ready for the wedding. They had agreed to let everything that had happened go and just start fresh as they began to prepare for their new life together. Karl had never seen the note coming.

He had been furious the first week. Occasionally, something would go flying across the room as he recalled all the signs that had always been there, flashing red that they weren't a good match. When he realized his anger was too much, he left the bookstore for good and trusted Janice to finish closing it out.

Before too long, his anger changed into relief as he became grateful that they didn't get married. He realized he never would have been happy with things always having to go her way. Felicia had shown she needed the comfort of money to live on, not the love of a simple man.

Karl shook his head as he drove. How had they ever become a couple in the first place? Karl had always been a simple man wanting simple things, no matter the amount of money in his pocket. It turned out that his family's money was what Felicia found attractive.

Felicia, his family's money, and his dad were all gone. He could handle losing the store and Felicia, but losing his dad was another story. Karl could always find a new girlfriend somewhere way down the road, and he could make back some, if not all, of the money he lost by selling the store. But there wasn't a single way to bring his dad back.

He slammed his hand on the steering wheel. Karl still couldn't wrap his head around his father being gone. In the beginning, Karl had blamed Michael. He knew it was wrong to do that, but when Karl found out everything that had gone on, he felt like the stress Michael had caused was the culprit of his dad's heart attack. It turned out that Peter's heart had been unhealthy for a while. He just hadn't told anyone so they wouldn't worry.

That was their dad, though, always thinking of others. Judy admitted that she knew his heart wasn't good toward the end. She had made him tell her one day after he returned home from a doctor's appointment with prescriptions. So Karl stopped blaming Michael, but he didn't stop blaming God.

Karl looked at the mountains surrounding Autumnville as he entered the city limits. How could a God that created something so majestic be so willing to take a loved one away too soon?

"Well, God, if you're there anymore, it sure would be nice if you could show me what I'm supposed to do now," Karl turned onto the street leading to Stacy's house.

CHAPTER EIGHTEEN

"Uncle Karl!" Nicole screamed as she came running out of Stacy's house.

Karl picked up his niece and hugged her tightly. His nephew, Ben, was out the door and hugging Karl's leg a second later. Karl ruffled Ben's hair as he put Nicole down. Stacy joined them as Karl scooped Ben up into a hug. Karl loved his five-year-old niece and three-year-old nephew like they were his own.

Once he put Ben down and hugged Stacy, Karl grabbed his bag from the passenger side of his truck and went inside with everyone.

"Is Uncle Karl sleeping in my room?" Ben asked.

"Yes, why don't you go show Uncle Karl your new bed?" Stacy suggested.

"You got a new bed!" Karl acted excited for Ben, sensing it was a big deal. "I can't wait to see it!"

"Come on, I'll show you," Ben tugged Karl's hand to go upstairs. Ben's room had been the guest room until he was old enough to sleep by himself. Stacy and John had replaced the full-size bed with twin oak bunk beds. The quaint decorations that usually welcomed any guests had been replaced with toys and furniture perfect for little boys.

"Wow, Ben, your room looks great!" Karl put his bag on the top bunk. "Do I get the top bunk?"

Ben pouted his lips. "Yeah, Mom says I'm not old enough for it yet."

"Well, bottom bunks are cool too," Karl said.

"They are?" Bens eyes widened with hope for a good answer.

"Well, sure," Karl said, having to think quickly. "They're easier to get out of if you have to go to the bathroom at night."

Ben thought for a minute but seemed okay with the answer. He went to one of his toy boxes and pulled out some trucks and cars to play with.

"Let's play!" he told Karl.

"We will later, okay, buddy," Karl said. "Right now, I need to hang out with your mom for a bit."

Karl found Stacy downstairs in the kitchen working on supper.

"Whatever you're cooking smells delicious," he told her as he took a seat at the bar.

Stacy put a casserole dish in the oven and set the timer. "Chicken and rice," she put dirty dishes in the dishwasher and cleaned the counter.

"Can I help with anything?" Karl asked.

"No," Stacy went to the fridge to get items needed for a salad. "I love cooking and prepping. I find it therapeutic."

"You should have been a chef instead of a nurse."

"No, I don't think I would enjoy cooking as much if it were a career," Stacy responded. "It's good to have something that takes your mind off things."

Karl knew what was coming, but he asked anyway, "What's on your mind, Sis?"

CHAPTER NINETEEN

By the time Karl went to bed later that evening, he was exhausted. Between having to admit to everything he'd been feeling and thinking since February and playing with the kids, Karl was wiped out.

Stacy was the only one that could get Karl to be completely honest about how he was doing. Ever since they were kids and Karl started having to take on roles Michael should have, he had kept how he was doing to himself. For him, everyone else's well-being was more important.

Stacy had this amazing ability of knowing when Karl wasn't okay. She called it her "sister sense." When she had a "sense" about things, she didn't let up until he talked. Maybe that's why it worked so well—everyone else gave up, but she didn't. That's how Karl ended up in her kitchen. Stacy hadn't let up until she had cornered him into coming for a visit.

As Karl tried to climb up the ladder to the top bunk without waking Ben, he heard Ben shift in his bed.

"Good night, Uncle Karl," Ben spoke softly.

"Good night, Ben."

"I love you, Uncle Karl."

Karl looked down into Ben's bed at the boy talking in his sleep. "I love you, too, Ben."

Karl spent the next couple of days helping John with yard work. He enjoyed the physical labor, his muscles screaming from lack of use. He spent the afternoons swimming with the kids in the family's aboveground pool and the evenings at the ballpark watching Nicole play T-ball.

By the end of the week, Karl noticed his body was the most relaxed it had been since his mom's phone call back in February. He was eating breakfast with Stacy and the kids when Stacy suggested they go downtown to the bookstore. Karl was surprisingly apprehensive.

"They have a great children's program during the summer," Stacy told him.

"I wouldn't mind walking downtown while you guys do that," Karl answered. He knew he had to at least go with them, but he hoped he could avoid actually going into the store.

Thirty minutes later, Stacy parked her SUV in front of Autumn Nook Bookstore. Karl spotted a coffee shop down the block and decided that was the perfect escape.

"Hey, Sis," Karl said as they all rolled out of the car, "I'm going to go get a coffee while you guys are in the bookstore. I'll meet you after you're done." He quickly walked off, not giving Stacy a chance to respond.

Once inside Flavour, Karl was relieved to see a line at the counter. It would delay him even longer. He felt his phone vibrate in the back pocket of his shorts. He knew before opening the text that it was from Stacy.

"Why are you avoiding the bookstore?" she asked.

"I'm not."

"Yes, you are."

Karl put his phone up as the line moved forward.

"Good morning, Mr. Lovewell," Karl heard the cashier say to the man in front of him.

"Good morning, Sally," the man responded. "How's your mom doing today?"

"Good as could be expected," Sally admitted. "She's enjoying the books though."

"I'm glad to hear that," Mr. Lovewell took a bag from under his arm and handed it to Sally. "Here's some more for her. I included a new author I'd like to get her thoughts on."

"Oh, Mr. Lovewell," Sally's eyes glistened, "please let me pay you for these. There's at least fifty dollars in books there."

"No, Sally, I won't let you pay for them. That's one of the perks of owning the bookstore."

Karl was frozen in place as David Lovewell moved aside so Karl could place his order.

"Can I help you, Sir?" Sally asked Karl.

Karl couldn't believe what he had just witnessed. It reminded him so much of the things his dad would do to help people and his community. Karl tried to hold his emotions in check while he ordered a regular coffee. As he and David stood there waiting for their coffees, Karl tried hard not to stare at David. It was the first time since his father passed away that Karl was reminded that kindness and good people still existed.

Sally handed both of them their coffees. As David took his, he said, "You tell your mom to let me know what she thinks of the new author."

"I sure will, Mr. Lovewell," Sally said.

Karl and David walked out of the coffee shop at the same time. "Do you do that a lot?" Karl started.

"Do what?" David asked.

"Give your books away," Karl said matter-of-factly.

"Well," David started as they fell into step with each other, "it depends on the situation. I grew up with Sally's mom. She's losing the battle against breast cancer and can't hardly get out of bed now. Why do you ask?"

Karl felt himself shrink a little as he heard David's answer. "I…I just wondered," Karl said. "My dad used to do those types of things, too, when he was alive."

"Oh, was he from here?" David asked.

"No, he lived in Shale, New York," Karl answered.

"Oh, are you related to Stacy Peterson?" David asked.

"Yes, I'm her brother," Karl said. "How do you know her?"

"We attend the same church," David said as they came up to the bookstore. "I'm very sorry for your loss." David put his hand on the store door.

Karl hesitated slightly and then motioned toward the store. "Stacy and the kids are actually here right now."

"Well," David pulled open the door, "let's go see what mess the kids are all making today."

Meeting David had been a much needed turning point for Karl. He had spent the entire afternoon talking and hanging out with David after meeting him at the coffee shop. It had been nice to be able to talk to someone who understood bookstore stuff. Karl returned to the bookstore every day to talk to David. After a couple of visits, David offered Karl a job as his manager.

At first Karl had said no because he didn't want to be pitied. David assured Karl that wasn't the case at all. David had been passively looking for someone to help him run the store and felt Karl had been an answer to prayer.

Karl went back to Spires, packed up his apartment, and notified his landlord he was breaking his lease. Two weeks later, Karl settled into his new two-bedroom house just a couple of miles from Stacy. It had been on the market long enough that when Karl made a cash offer way under the asking price, the seller had agreed.

It was his first day working at Autumn Nook. Karl was excited to be getting back into a bookstore. He hadn't been sure he would ever be able to enter one again. He had thought his next job wouldn't have anything to do with books. While he didn't own Autumn Nook, he was excited to help run it. He was curious how or if David did things differently than his dad had.

CHAPTER TWENTY

Karl couldn't believe the Christmas season was almost upon them. He was enjoying his new life in Autumnville. It was nice to help Stacy and John with the kids when he could. Most weekends, the kids stayed over at his place, and that was quickly becoming one of his favorite things. He was also getting involved in their church and making a lot of great friends in the community. In some ways, Karl was enjoying life more than he had when he owned the store in Spires. Judy and Michael had even come for a visit once to see his new place and the kids.

Karl and David were discussing what sales to do for Halloween and Thanksgiving. Karl soaked up David's business knowledge, and he learned snippets about David over lunches, during coffee breaks, and at events at church.

He was surprised how many people didn't seem to like David, but Karl couldn't figure out why. David had a very compassionate heart and truly cared about others, but a lot of the older people in town seemed to have something against him, not that it mattered to Karl. David was helping him complete the grieving process for his dad.

David's phone lit up briefly on his desk. Karl glanced at it and noticed a picture of a woman on the screen.

"Who's that?" Karl asked pointing at the phone as he remembered that David didn't have any family.

David picked up the phone so Karl could see the picture better. The woman had shoulder-length auburn hair and green eyes. Karl thought she was very pretty.

"This is Emma," David said. "I told you about her before. She's like a daughter to me."

"Oh, she lives in Texas, right?" Karl asked.

"Yeah, I don't get to see her often," David said. "Now, what do you think about marking these books down and putting them on the front table until after Thanksgiving?"

Karl noticed the quick change in topic and took his cue to help David make a decision about the sales. He was looking forward to Halloween and going trick-or-treating with Nicole and Ben.

Before Karl knew it, Halloween was over, and he was helping John wrap the house in white Christmas lights the day after Thanksgiving. He was looking forward to celebrating the holiday in Autumnville. Judy and Michael were coming down for Christmas also. This would be the first time the whole family celebrated Christmas at Stacy's house. Christmas was always done at his parent's house, but Karl understood his mom not wanting to do that this year with Dad gone.

Christmas was a solemn affair. Everyone felt the loss of Peter. It was hard to celebrate and share memories without bringing up Peter. There wasn't a dry eye among them. Even Nicole and Ben felt the loss of their grandfather. They all did their best to endure it, though, and to create new memories. By the end of the evening, tears had been replaced with laughter and everyone was enjoying the holiday a little more.

CHAPTER TWENTY-ONE

It was the second weekend in January. Nicole and Ben were hanging out at Karl's place while Stacy worked a late shift at the hospital. John was out of town on a business trip and due to be back on Sunday. The kids had settled in on the couch to watch a movie while Karl made hot dogs for dinner. There was a light knock on the front door. When Karl went to answer it, he found Stacy standing on the other side.

"Stacy?" Karl said. "What are you doing here so early? I thought you had to work until midnight."

Karl realized as he spoke that Stacy didn't look okay. Her eyes were wide and shining like she had been crying, her face blotched with red patches.

"Stacy, what's wrong?" he coaxed his sister inside.

"John," was all Stacy could say.

Karl helped Stacy out of her coat and led her into the kitchen, hoping the kids wouldn't see her. Karl had Stacy sit down while he poured her a glass of water. He sat on the chair next to her as he gave her the glass.

"What about John?" he asked.

Stacy looked at Karl. "He's dead."

"What?" Karl grabbed Stacy's arms. He realized she was in shock. "Tell me what happened."

"It was a drunk driver. He ran the stop sign and hit John's car so hard it flipped over several times before coming to a stop. The police officer said John's neck broke while the car was rolling."

"Oh, Stacy, I'm so sorry." Karl stood up, bringing Stacy with him and pulling her into a hug.

"How do I tell the kids? How do I explain that their dad isn't coming home?" she said, breaking down.

Karl held his sister until she calmed down.

"What's burning?" she asked.

"Oh, man," Karl went to the stove to turn the hot dogs off. "That was supposed to be our supper."

Nicole and Ben came running into the kitchen.

"Uncle Karl…" Nicole said, "Mom, what are you doing here?"

Stacy looked at Karl.

"Let's all go into the living room for a bit," Karl said. "I'll be there in a minute."

Stacy lingered. "What are you doing?" she asked as Karl took his phone out of his pocket.

"I'm going to order a pizza, and then we'll go tell the kids about John."

Three hours later, Karl carried Nicole's and Ben's sleeping bodies to his spare bedroom and tucked them into the full-size bed. He grabbed an extra blanket from the closet and tucked Stacy in on the couch, where she had fallen asleep. Karl, however, was wide awake.

He didn't know how to take the news about John's death. He didn't understand why God had let it happen so soon after everything else. Karl had thought things were getting better. He was happy again.

Of course, the counselor he was seeing helped. Karl had started going to therapy right before Christmas. While he was okay for the most part, he couldn't let go of his anger. Dr. Marrow was helping him with that. Together, they figured out his anger stemmed from things he couldn't control, like his father's death, losing the bookstore, and losing Felicia.

Karl still couldn't bring himself to admit he was angry mostly at God. In his inability to understand, Karl blamed God for not taking care of him and his family. With Stacy's husband was gone, her kids were without a father. Why did God keep letting these things happen?

Karl threw the kitchen towel he'd been using to wipe off the counter and table. He was about fed up with God if this was what God viewed as best for him and those he loved. As far as he was concerned, God could just butt out!

CHAPTER TWENTY-TWO

Karl's phone buzzed beside his bed, jarring him awake. He glanced at the clock as he answered it. It was two in the morning.

"Hello," Karl said sleepily.

"Hey, Karl," Stacy said from the other side of the connection. "I'm sorry, but Ben's having another nightmare."

"I'll be right over."

Six weeks had passed since John's death. Stacy was doing the best she could as a single mom. Nicole had become a great helper to Stacy and Ben was doing his best, but he was having trouble sleeping at night. It was becoming routine for Stacy to call during the night, asking Karl to come over to help calm Ben down. For some reason, Ben only responded to Karl's attempt at waking him up.

Karl was at Stacy's house within twenty minutes. It took almost an hour to get Ben calmed down and back to sleep. Stacy walked Karl to the front door.

Karl hesitated as he slipped on his jacket. "He needs to see a counselor. He doesn't know how to grieve John's death."

"No, Karl," Stacy said sharply. "I think he'll be fine. We just have to let him get through this."

Karl threw his hands up in defense. "Sis, I'm not going to tell you what to do. It was just a suggestion."

Stacy's tone softened. "I know, Karl. I'm just not ready to go that route." She hugged Karl, "Try to get some sleep before you have to go to work."

Karl went home, crawled into bed, and flipped on the TV. This was becoming his norm on nights like these. He was wide awake, and it was only four in the morning. His mind rambled as he stared at the TV. He wished Stacy would take Ben to see a counselor, but he knew better than to interfere. As he started to doze off, he prayed Stacy would come around about counseling.

The weather was finally warm enough to take the kids to the park. Karl was pushing Nicole and Ben on the swings when he noticed David sitting on a bench nearby. Once they were going pretty good, Karl left the kids swinging and went over to David.

"I love you, too, Emma. I'll talk to you soon," David was saying as Karl walked up. "Hey, it's a good day to swing," David said to Karl as he motioned toward Nicole and Ben.

"Yeah, the kids needed it," Karl sat down next to David.

"I'm sure you needed it too," David added.

"Yeah, it is a nice break from things, but I didn't expect to see you here."

"Oh, I thought I would enjoy the sunshine for a while before returning to work." David winked as he added, "Someone has to run the store, you know."

"Is everything okay?" Karl asked.

"Everything is fine, Karl," David spoke slowly. "We are going to have to make some changes though."

Karl's back stiffened. "What kind of changes?" He needed his world to stop erupting.

"Relax, Karl," David started, "all I mean is you're going to be head man at the store for a while."

Karl gave him a questioning look as they sat in silence for a bit. When David finally spoke, Karl couldn't believe what he was hearing.

"I'm dying, Karl," David sighed. "I have lung cancer, and it's too far progressed to waste money on treatment."

Karl recalled how David didn't seem to have the energy he did when they had first met. Come to think of it, David had been looking pale for about a month, but even knowing the signs had been there, it still made Karl angry.

"Don't be angry, Karl," David said.

Karl was shocked that anger had shown on his face.

"There's nothing for you to be angry about," David continued.

"Oh, I don't know about that," Karl said. "It seems all God ever does now is take away. There's never anything good happening anymore."

David laughed lightly.

"What's so funny?" Karl asked.

"You and Emma," David replied between laughs. "You're both so quick to blame God that you miss what He's doing."

"Huh?" was all Karl could say.

"Karl, your father and John didn't die as a way to intentionally hurt you," David began. "He didn't take away the bookstore because He didn't love you. Same thing with Felicia. No, Karl, He did all that *because* He loves you."

"That's a harsh way to show love, isn't it?" Karl griped.

"Well, yes," David answered, "but look at what has come of it. You're in a new place. You're happier here." David pointed toward the swing set. "You're helping your sister and getting to know your niece and nephew. Whether you realize it or not, God did everything to place you here, now, right where He needs you."

"You really think all that's true?" Karl asked.

"Yes," David replied, "because I believe He brought you to me. I'm going to need you to teach Emma how to run the bookstore."

THE END

COMING SOON

"EMMA'S JOURNEY"

BOOK 2 OF THE AUTUMNVILLE SERIES

What do you do when your friend wills you a destiny?

The death of Emma Chandler's friend and mentor devastated her almost as much as finding out about his past. But when she learns his plans for her in his small hometown, she will have to make hard decisions about who she is, what she believes, and the man she's falling for.

ABOUT THE AUTUMNVILLE SERIES

Autumnville, North Carolina is a small town buried deep in faith. To outsiders, it's just your typical, small, sleepy town. Once you pass the city limit sign, however, something magically medicinal begins to take place. All who visit are transformed as they experience an awakening.

About the Author

K Wendt resides with her family in Central Texas. She is an award winning, multi-genre author who enjoys creating stories for readers of all ages. Along with writing, she also coaches authors through writing projects, and presents workshops for breaking down the creative block. K enjoys lazy weekends with her family and reading a good book. You can follow her on her website www.ksbooknook.com for upcoming book releases and events.

OTHER BOOKS BY THIS AUTHOR

CHILDREN'S BOOKS

Duney

Susie

Billy

Danny

Julie

Susie and Friends Coloring Book

Washed Away

Bunny in the Bluebonnets

Phoebe

Jack the Jackrabbit

Where Did My Stars Go?

FICTION BOOKS

Karl's Passage

Emma's Journey

Burned on Sunday

POETRY BOOKS

Beneath it All

Just a Doodle

WORKBOOKS

Why I Write

Why I Create

www.ingramcontent.com/pod-product-compliance
Lightning Source LLC
Chambersburg PA
CBHW022051170626
46808CB00003B/1435